Kings and Queens

Subhadra Sen Gupta has written over thirty books for children including mysteries, historical adventures, ghost stories, comic books and books on history. To her surprise, the Sahitya Akademi thinks she is doing a good job and gave her the Bal Sahitya Puraskar 2014. Right now she is waiting for a time machine so that she can travel to the past and join Emperor Akbar for lunch. She loves to travel, flirt with cats and chat with auto-rickshaw drivers. If you want to discuss anything under the sun with her, email her at subhadrasg@gmail.com

Tapas Guha has been working for more than twenty years as an illustrator. He has worked with many leading publishers, newspapers, advertising agencies and NGOs. He loves to draw comics and illustrate children's books. He has partnered with Subhadra Sen Gupta on countless projects including a Feluda comics series. Ruskin Bond is one of his favourite authors and he loves to read Tintin comics.

EXPLORING INDIA

Kings and Queens

SUBHADRA SEN GUPTA

Illustrated by **TAPAS GUHA**

RED TURTLE
RUPA

Published in Red Turtle by
Rupa Publications India Pvt. Ltd 2016
7/16, Ansari Road, Daryaganj
New Delhi 110002

Sales centres:
Allahabad Bengaluru Chennai
Hyderabad Jaipur Kathmandu
Kolkata Mumbai

Text Copyright © Subhadra Sen Gupta 2016
Illustrations Copyright © Rupa Publications 2016

The views and opinions expressed in this book are the author's own and the facts are as reported by her which have been verified to the extent possible, and the publishers are not in any way liable for the same.

All rights reserved.
No part of this publication may be reproduced, transmitted, or stored in a retrieval system, in any form or by any means, electronic, mechanical, photocopying, recording or otherwise, without the prior permission of the publisher.

ISBN: 978-81-291-3758-6

First impression 2016

10 9 8 7 6 5 4 3 2 1

The moral right of the author has been asserted.

Printed at IPP Ltd, Noida

This book is sold subject to the condition that it shall not,
by way of trade or otherwise, be lent, resold, hired out,
or otherwise circulated, without the publisher's prior consent,
in any form of binding or cover other than that
in which it is published.

Contents

Introduction / vii

CHANDRAGUPTA MAURYA / 1
(Reign 321 BCE–297 BCE)

RAZIA SULTAN / 21
(Reign 1336–1340 CE)

KRISHNADEVA RAYA / 37
(Reign 1509–1529 CE)

NURJAHAN / 61
(Reign 1611–1627 CE)

Introduction

What makes a monarch great?

We have all heard about famous kings like the emperors Ashoka and Akbar. However, have you ever wondered why they are called 'Great'?

There are some unique qualities of character that transform a mere king to one who is called great. Oddly enough, there are also quite a few other Indian kings and queens who had many of these qualities but were never given that title. Here we tell you the story of two kings and two queens who stand out among the crowded pages of our long history because of their courage, ability and their exciting lives.

In ancient times, a king had to be, first of all, a great warrior and general who could lead an army, build a kingdom and then defend it against enemies. He also had to be a hard-working ruler who knew how to keep his subjects happy. If there was peace in the kingdom then agriculture, industry and trade would flourish. This meant that the king could collect more taxes which could be used to run the kingdom. To be a great king, they had to rule over prosperous empires.

The most successful rulers made sure there was law and order in their kingdoms so that peace prevailed. Then they built roads, bridges, irrigation canals and dams in order to improve people's lives. They were interested in culture and encouraged writers, poets, musicians and painters. They were also great patrons of art, literature and architecture, and built beautiful palaces and fortresses.

Finally, there is one important quality that all great Indian rulers share. They were tolerant monarchs who held no prejudice about religion. In their reigns, you were judged by your abilities and not your faith. They all understood that in a land like India with so many religions, the only way to keep their subjects united and their kingdoms peaceful was by treating every religion with equal respect.

So in this book you will read about two very unusual kings and two queens—courageous, hard-working, tolerant leaders who genuinely cared for their subjects. The queens had an additional burden—they had to battle the prejudices of society against female rulers.

So let's read about Chandragupta Maurya, Razia Sultan, Krishnadeva Raya and Nurjahan. They may not have been as great as Ashoka or Akbar but they were all wonderful rulers who led eventful and colourful lives.

CHANDRAGUPTA MAURYA

(Reign 321 BCE–297 BCE)

He was the son of a poor widow, who was brought up by a cowherd and educated by a Brahmin scholar named Chanakya. He may have met the Greek conqueror Alexander. This remarkable boy went on to establish India's first empire. If we didn't know it was all true, we'd think someone made up the story.

Chandragupta Maurya became the king of Magadha and ruled from Pataliputra that was one of the greatest cities of the ancient world. He was a warrior and king who founded the Mauryan dynasty. It is possible that he had a Greek wife and incidentally, he was also Emperor Ashoka's grandfather. And he achieved all this over 2,000 years ago.

Early life

Chandragupta's life reads like a breathtaking adventure tale. No one really knows much about his birth and historians have tried to patch the story of his origin together from many sources. We find many legends about him in our ancient texts like the Puranas, Buddhist and Jain chronicles. There is also a play written in the ninth century CE called *Mudra Rakshasa* by Visakhadatta about a king called Chandragupta and his rise to power. This work of drama provides details of palace intrigue by a clever Brahmin named Chanakya and so it is probably based on true events.

In ancient times, writing history was not a very precise

art and writers included everything from legends and hearsay to imaginary stories, somewhat like our modern-day film gossip magazines. However they all agree that Chandragupta was not of royal birth. Some say he was the son of the chieftain of a Kshatriya clan called Moriya that ruled at a place called Pipphalivana. Others write that he was the son of a dead Nanda king but as his mother was a low caste woman called Mura, he could not claim the throne. The Jain texts say he was the son of the chieftain of a tribe of peacock breeders who were called mayura poshaka. It's sort of fun to think that maybe the dynasty was named after the magnificent peacock!

Chandragupta and his mother lived in a poor locality of Pataliputra and he was brought up first by a cowherd and then a hunter. One day, he was playing with his friends in the lane, a bunch of barefoot boys play-acting as kings and noblemen. They didn't notice a Brahmin who was going past and had stopped to watch. The scene being enacted was a royal court and Chandragupta was playing the king. As he sat yelling out commands to his ragged bunch of friends, the Brahmin was impressed by the boy's cleverness and leadership skills.

This Brahmin was called Chanakya or Kautilya and he observed something in the boy that made him take on Chandragupta as a student. Chanakya was a teacher in far-off Takshashila (modern Taxila, Pakistan) in the north-west. Takshashila was then a great centre of learning where Chanakya taught at a university. Chandragupta was taken there, educated and also trained as a warrior. In fact he was being groomed for kingship and it was clear Chanakya had a reason for adopting Chandragupta.

The Brahmin was planning revenge against the most powerful dynasty of the land—the Nandas of Magadha. At that time, Magadha was ruled by Dhana Nanda of Pataliputra and Chanakya had once been accused of theft, insulted in public and banished by him. Chanakya threw a tantrum, untied his shikha, that long braid of hair that Brahmins wore and vowed that he would not tie it again till he had his revenge. The problem was that he was no warrior and that's where Chandragupta came in.

Dhana Nanda was a cruel and greedy man who was unpopular with his subjects as he taxed them heavily and hoarded his gold. Some said that he had hidden his treasures in an underground cave in the Ganga River. So Chanakya knew that the people would welcome a saviour.

So young Chandragupta, penniless and without an army or a kingdom, was expected by his guru to take on the most powerful king of the land and win.

Oh great one, Alexander!

In 327 BCE, Chandragupta was still studying in Takshashila

when the Greek army of Alexander the Great swept in from Afghanistan and entered Punjab. Alexander defeated King Pururava (King Porus) by the banks of the Jhelum River, occupied Takshashila, the capital of King Ambhi (King Omphis) and planned to move further east. Then, by the banks of the Beas River, his triumphant progress came to a halt as he faced a mutiny. His soldiers refused to proceed as they were tired of fighting and wanted to go home. So an angry Alexander headed back to Greece but died on the way at Babylon in 323 BCE. One Greek historian wrote that the Greek soldiers had also mutinied because they were scared of fighting the army of Dhana Nanda.

There is a legend that Chandragupta went to Alexander seeking his help against Dhana Nanda but he was refused. The Roman historian Plutarch says that Alexander met a 'Sandrocottos' who wanted his support against Magadha but the Greek king was not impressed and turned the man away. When he left India, Alexander appointed governors called Satraps to rule the land he had conquered and among them were Pururava, Ambhi and a Greek named Seleucus Nicator. One day, Chandragupta would meet Seleucus on the battlefield and it would lead to a man named Megasthenes being sent as an ambassador to Chandragupta's court and he would wander around Magadha like a modern-day tourist and write a book.

Target Dhana Nanda

Chandragupta and Chanakya had learnt one important lesson from Alexander's small Greek force defeating Pururava's giant army which was made up of archers, chariots and hundreds of elephants. They realized that a smaller but better disciplined army and a clever battle strategy can defeat a bigger force. So they concluded that with the right plan they could take on Magadha.

Chandragupta collected an army with the help of local kings and conquered Punjab and Sindh and then moved towards Magadha. Sadly, his campaign against the Nandas turned out to be a disaster. Filled with confidence after his early success, Chandragupta marched straight towards Pataliputra and was surrounded and defeated by the giant Nanda army. With his soldiers dead or scattered, Chandragupta barely managed to escape with his life and the story goes that he had to hide in a village from Dhana Nanda's men.

A despondent Chandragupta was sitting by a village hut when he saw a woman serve a plate of piping hot rice and dal to her son. The boy was hungry and immediately placed his hand in the middle of the mound of rice crying out as it scalded his fingers. The mother scolded him saying he should never start from the middle where the rice is the hottest but from the edges where it had already cooled.

8 KINGS AND QUEENS

So a plate of rice gave Chandragupta his battle plan. He went back to Punjab and with another army he began to attack the borders of the Nanda kingdom. He would capture the frontier towns and fortresses that were guarded by small garrisons, consolidate his position and then move inwards towards the heart of the kingdom till one day, in 321 BCE, his soldiers swept into Pataliputra and defeated Dhana Nanda.

As Chanakya had hoped, the people came out to welcome Chandragupta and he was crowned monarch. And what happened to mean old Dhana Nanda? The man who had hoarded a fabulous treasure was allowed to leave with what he could pack into one chariot. Chanakya had his revenge and Chandragupta had won himself a kingdom. So Chanakya's shikha was now tied up again.

Chandragupta had won an unequal battle. His army was a ragtag band of tribal warriors, mercenaries, hill men and even bandits. According to the Roman historian Curtius, the Nanda army had 20,000 cavalry, 2 lakh infantry, 2,000 four-horse chariots and 300 elephants! Even if he was exaggerating, which is often the case with historians of ancient times, the Nanda army had foot soldiers, horsemen, archers, chariots and elephants in large numbers. Luckily, Dhana Nanda was a disaster as a general and Chandragupta was a crafty, battle-hardened warrior and in such wars leadership makes a crucial difference.

10 KINGS AND QUEENS

Pick up your sword

Even after he had become king, Chandragupta never stopped the military campaigns, as if he had an unending hunger for land. Within a few years a large part of India came under his control and it grew into the largest kingdom in the Indian subcontinent. His empire spread from modern Bengal to east Afghanistan, north to Kashmir and south till Karnataka. However, we don't know much about his various conquests, except for his war against the Greek king Seleucus Nicator.

At Alexander's death, his generals had divided up his empire and so, many regions in Asia and Africa now had Greek kings. Egypt had gone to Ptolemy (his descendant Cleopatra, queen of Egypt, was in fact hundred per cent Greek). Seleucus's share was the land from Persia to the banks of the Indus and he soon came into conflict with Chandragupta who had conquered Punjab.

Seleucus and Chandragupta met on the battlefield in 305 BCE. The Greek historians do not provide any details of the battle probably because the Greeks lost but the terms of the treaty show clearly that Chandagupta had triumphed over the Macedonian army. By the treaty Seleucus gave up Herat, Kandahar and Kabul in Afghanistan and in return Chandragupta magnanimously gifted him with 500 elephants. Getting a large chunk of Afghanistan in exchange for a few elephants? Clearly it was Chandragupta who was dictating the terms of the treaty which also mentions a matrimonial alliance. So it's possible either Chandragupta or one of his sons married a Greek princess and maybe Ashoka had a Greek grandmother. How cool is that?

A Greek in Pataliputra

Imagine a Greek in a knee-length tunic wandering around the city that we now call Patna. The most interesting result of the Seleucus-Chandragupta encounter was that the Greek king sent an ambassador named Megasthenes to Pataliputra and he turned out to be one of the first travel writers of the world. Megasthenes wrote a memoir of his travels called *Indika*. The actual book is lost but luckily large parts were quoted by later Greek and Roman historians like Arrian, Strabo and Diodorus. We get a pretty good description of the city and the life of the people from his writings.

Most interesting are his descriptions of Pataliputra and the life of not just royalty but also ordinary people. Megasthenes called the city 'Palimbothra' and the king 'Sandrocottos' and it was only in the nineteenth century that the great historian and linguist William Jones made the connection that Sandrocottos was Chandragupta. Then he matched the geographical descriptions of Palimbothra and realized it was modern Patna and so ancient Pataliputra.

Jones's discovery made a very important contribution to

12 KINGS AND QUEENS

Indian history—we finally had some real dates! You see our traditional historians just mention the year of a king's reign and so they would say, 'After five years of Chandragupta's reign...' which really gives you no idea when the event took place. What we did have now, was the exact dates by the Western calendar of Alexander's conquests in India and from there Jones made all the connections and finally we knew when all these exciting events took place.

Megasthenes got a bit confused at times like when he said Indian society had seven castes and that there was no slavery in the land. He probably mixed up professions with varna or caste when he listed them as philosophers, farmers, soldiers, herdsmen, artisans, magistrates and councillors. Also, Indians did keep slaves though they were different from Greek slaves who worked in farms and industry. Indian slaves were usually domestic servants. Megasthenes describes a prosperous society and mentions that the people had enough food and, 'were well skilled in the arts, as might be expected of men who inhale a pure air and drink the very finest water.' Clearly our man liked living in Pataliputra.

Megasthenes was very impressed by the magnificent city that stood on the confluence of the rivers Ganga and Sone. Pataliputra was surrounded by a high palisade made of thick logs of wood and a deep moat. Soldiers guarded the wall and could aim their spears and arrows through loopholes cut out in the wood. There were sixty-four gates and 570 towers and many of the gates were high enough for elephants to pass through. The gates were all closed at nightfall, the drawbridges would be raised and so if you came to the gate at night you had to wait outside.

Megasthenes was dazzled by the royal processions when Chandragupta rode out of his palace in a golden palanquin decorated with pearls. The king wore lots of jewellery and his clothes  were made of the finest muslin embellished in purple and gold. His palanquin was guarded by women bodyguards and the procession was made up of caparisoned elephants, four-horse chariots, tamed wild animals, marching soldiers and, interestingly, men carrying branches of trees with tame parrots trained to fly around the king. Chandragupta's palace was set within beautiful gardens and parks with fish pools. Megasthenes describes how the palace was, 'adorned with gilded pillars clasped all round with a vine embossed in gold and silver images of birds.'

14 KINGS AND QUEENS

Chanakya's Shastra

The Mauryan kingdom was very big but why do we call it an empire? An empire spans a much larger area and people of different races and speaking different languages live in it. It has many cities and there is great architecture. An empire is divided into provinces and governors are appointed to administer them. The Mauryan Empire had provinces like Avantika (Madhya Pradesh), Koshala (Uttar Pradesh), Takshashila (Punjab, Pakistan), Anga (eastern India) and Gandhara (Afghanistan).

Running such a huge empire at a time when they had no telephones, email, cars, trucks or railways was not easy. It needed a very efficient central administration and we get an idea how it was done from a book called *Arthasastra* that was written by Chanakya. The book talks about how a king could build and run an empire and grow in wealth and power.

Arthasastra is about the science of state craft, an efficient and ruthless system of administration. Chanakya was a political strategist and administrator who suggested how to collect revenue, control the bureaucracy, maintain an army and have a department of spies. He even offered advice on how to catch corrupt officials, so it looks like we have had this problem for 2,000 years! The book mentions a benevolent despot and says that the king was not just a

CHANDRAGUPTA MAURYA 15

conqueror and tax collector; he was also responsible for the welfare of his subjects and says, 'In the happiness of the subjects lies the happiness of the king.'

The Mauryan administration comprised of different departments managed by ministers called mahamatyas headed by the amatya or Chief Minister. The biggest expenses were the standing army and the salary of the bureaucracy and so the taxes had to be collected strictly. A census of the population was done, the first in India and everyone from farmers to crafts people and merchants were taxed.

It was a very prosperous empire with earnings from land revenue, taxes from traders and also Magadha had iron mines and the use of iron tools meant that everything from agriculture to crafts

improved. The land tax was either one-fourth or one-sixth of the produce and it was called bhaga. The land in every village was surveyed and taxed according to the crops it yielded.

By then, India was trading along the Silk Road with Rome and Egypt in the west and China and Burma in the east; sending cotton textiles, spices, metalware and even the famous Northern Black Polished pottery of Magadha and ghee! Highways connected cities, like the road called Dakshinapatha that ran from Pataliputra to the ports in Gujarat. Taxes paid for not just the army but also government salaries, building of roads and of course the expenses of the royal family that lived in great luxury.

Pataliputra was quite a cosmopolitan city and it had a separate government department to take care of foreigners. That means people from many countries must have visited the city. Megasthenes was the first Greek ambassador and later there were Deimakos from Syria during the reign of Bindusara and Dionysius while Ashoka was on the throne.

Walking away

Chandragupta was really a very unusual man. His rise to power was extraordinary and so was the way he gave it all up and walked away. During Mauryan times both Buddhism and Jainism were popular in India. Chandragupta was a

Jain and his guru was a scholar named Bhadrabahu. After twenty-four years as king, he faced a new kind of challenge. The empire was struck by years of drought and he decided to abdicate in favour of his son Bindusara.

In 297 BCE, Chandragupta donned the robes of a Jain monk, and accompanied by Bhadrabahu and other monks, began to proceed southwards. They stopped at a place in Karnataka called Sravana Belagola where Chandragupta chose Sallekhana—the Jain ritual of death by starvation. Today, on a hill in Sravana Belagola stands the famous stone image of the Jain saint Gomateshwara. Every twelve years this giant image is doused in milk, vermillion and saffron water in a colourful ceremony known as mahamastaka abhishekha.

Even after two millennia, people have not forgotten the king who finally became a monk. Nearby is a cave on a hill called Chandragiri where Chandragupta is said to have died and there is a temple here called Chandragupta Basadi. Interestingly, Chandragupta's grandson Ashoka first went on a campaign of conquest like him and then became a Buddhist, gave up war and through his Dhamma spread the word of peace and tolerance. Maybe somewhere he was listening to the voice of his extraordinary grandfather.

A Mauryan Mishmash

- The author of the *Arthasastra* is called by three names– Vishnugupta, which was probably his personal name; Kautilya was his gotra and Chanakya as he was the son of Chanaka.
- No historian of ancient India chronicles the invasion of Alexander. Megasthenes writes about Chandragupta but not of Chanakya. Then in *Arthasastra* Chanakya never mentions Chandragupta. Go figure!
- The Greeks really messed up the spellings of Indian names– Pururava became Porus, Ambhi was Omphis, Chandragupta became Sandrocottos, Pataliputra was Palimbothra and poor Bindusara became Amitradates.
- Greek historians narrated fantastic tales about India like giant ants that collected gold and human beings with no mouth, one eye and ears so large they used them as blankets! So no one believed them when they wrote about a plant that grew wool and another that produced a sweet syrup, when in fact they were describing cotton and sugarcane.
- The name Chandragupta was a popular choice for later kings and we have two more in the Gupta dynasty.
- What is truly weird is that Chandragupta Maurya became king in 321 BCE and Chandragupta I of the Gupta dynasty became king in 321 CE. Makes it easy to remember for the history tests!
- The *Arthasastra* was lost for centuries. In 1904, a palm leaf manuscript was handed over to R. Shamasastry, Chief

Librarian of Mysore by a Brahmin from Thanjavur. No one knows who that Brahmin was and why he donated the manuscript. The *Arthasastra* was discovered again as Shamasastry began to translate it into English.

Books You Can Read

1. *The Penguin History of Early India* by Romila Thapar; Penguin
2. *Ancient India* by R.C. Majumdar; Motilal Banarsidass
3. *A History of Ancient & Early Medieval India* by Upinder Singh; Pearson
4. *The Wonder That Was India* (Vol I) by A.L. Basham; Rupa

RAZIA SULTAN

(Reign 1336-1340 CE)

When you imagine an Indian queen you think of a pretty woman wearing a silk sari, a wobbly gold crown and tons of jewellery sitting silently beside her husband with a docile smile. This queen was different. She was the only woman who ever occupied the throne of Delhi and ruled as a sultan. Moreover, in spite of being a Muslim she did not wear a veil or remain quietly in the harem.

She liked to ride elephants and horses and she bravely marched out in battle at the head of her army and defeated her enemies. She was also the daughter of a slave and her father chose her as his successor even though he had living sons who could have gladly followed him on the throne. Razia Sultan may have ruled only for four years but we have never forgotten her.

The Slave kings

To understand Razia's life, we have to go back a few decades to the time when Delhi became a sultanate for the first time. A sultanate meant that the territory was now ruled by a Muslim sultan instead of a Hindu raja. Muslims had been living in India from much before this period. Till the last decades of the twelfth century, India had seen Muslims as merchants who came to the ports on the western coast and often settled at places like Kochi and Surat. Then a small Muslim kingdom did rise in the north-west in Sindh but the main Indian subcontinent was still governed by Hindu rulers. The sultanate was the first Muslim kingdom in mainland India. It was followed by the Mughal dynasty and this led to many changes in Indian society and culture.

India was known to be a rich country which had several Hindu temples that were laden with treasures and had often faced invasions by Muslim kings who used the excuse of religion to plunder and kill. The most notorious among them was Mahmud of Ghazni, who invaded India a number of times in the eleventh century and left the country in ruins. Fortunately, once he had collected a sizeable treasure he left soon after and went home. Muizuddin Muhammad bin Sam of Ghur, who also ruled from Ghazni in Afghanistan, was however, different.

Mohammad Ghur, to call him by a more convenient and shorter name, came to India with plans to stay and establish a kingdom. He fought two battles with Prithviraja Chauhan, the ruler of Ajmer in Rajasthan. In the first battle in 1191, Prithviraja won but for some strange reason he let Muhammad escape when he should have chased and captured him. Next year, Muhammad was back with a larger force and at the second battle of Tarain, Prithviraja was defeated and the Ghur troops entered Delhi. Muhammad Ghur had to go back to Ghazni so he appointed one of his trusted generals, Qutubuddin Aibak, as the governor of Delhi.

In 1205, while on his way back to Delhi Muhammad Ghur was stabbed to death. Muhammad did not have any sons and his trusted lieutenants were three former slaves one of them being Aibak. These three slaves divided up the kingdom of their patron and after fighting the other two, Aibak gained the Indian region.

Slaves becoming sultans, sounds strange, doesn't it? That is because we have this image of slaves being powerless people but in Asia it was quite different. Often soldiers captured as prisoners of war were made slaves but if they had talent and ability they were later freed and became officers and generals. Some even became kings, like the Mamluks of Egypt. Even the first dynasty of the Delhi Sultanate is called the Mamluk or the Slave dynasty and Razia belonged to this dynasty.

What is unusual is that the Slave dynasty had three men who were former slaves—Qutubuddin Aibak, his son-in-law Shamsuddin Iltutmish and later Ghiyas-ud-din Balban. Aibak had been sultan only for five years when he fell from his horse while playing polo and died. Soon after, Iltutmish became the next sultan in 1210. Razia was Iltutmish's eldest daughter and Aibak's granddaughter. So she had the bloodline to be a sultan, the only problem was that she was a woman.

A very unusual sultan

It was the early days of the dynasty and Iltutmish was battling at numerous fronts to establish a kingdom. Aibak had not been able to consolidate the kingdom and it fell to Iltutmish to do so. He had to first defeat the other slave generals of Muhammad Ghur who were also claiming the Indian kingdom. Then there were uprisings by Hindu rajas who wanted to reclaim Delhi. When Iltutmish began his reign, the Sultanate only held the region between Lahore and Delhi and he led expeditions to extend the boundaries of the kingdom eastwards towards Kanauj and Bengal. So he was often away from Delhi and when he left, he appointed young Razia as his deputy. In this way, she gained experience in running the kingdom.

In the beginning, the heir apparent was Iltutmish's eldest son Nasir-ud-din Mahmud but he passed away in 1229. The Sultanate did not have any established rule of succession which meant that there was a power struggle between the sons when a sultan died. Iltutmish wanted to avoid this but he did not trust any of his other sons and after much thought he nominated his eldest daughter Razia as his heir. Even in today's world that makes him a rare father.

When Iltutmish died in 1236, the kingdom was much larger and running smoothly but was it ready to be ruled by a woman? Were Razia's brothers and the members of the nobility going to allow her to claim the throne? Razia, however, was ready for the challenge.

Being a female sultan in thirteenth-century Delhi was going to be very, very tough. Razia's biggest problem was the powerful Muslim nobility. When the Sultanate was established in Delhi, Muslim men from Persia, Afghanistan, Central Asian countries and Turkey poured into India seeking work and many of them eventually rose to power. They became generals in the army, government officials and also large landowners. The sultans did not employ Hindus in high positions and so some of these men became ministers and were given titles like malik or noblemen.

These courtiers were divided into rival factions, all of them trying to gain power and influence with the sultan and become kingmakers. So the Turks were fighting the Afghans, the Persians conspiring against the Tajiks, and only a strong man like Iltutmish could control them. These power-hungry men wanted a weak sultan on the throne whom they could turn into a puppet and control. They were not keen to have an efficient and tough sultan who also happened to be a woman. So Razia knew she would have to fight these men to stay on the throne.

The medieval historian Ziauddin Barani mentions an ambitious and troublesome group of Turkish courtiers he calls chihalgani or the 'family of forty' who had no intention of letting Razia become the sultan. Neither did one of Iltutmish's queens called Shah Turkan who was the mother of Ruknuddin Firuz and planned to be the real power behind the throne. So the Forty and Turkan declared Firuz the sultan and Razia remained quiet.

Firuz proved to be a disaster as a king. He was quite happy to let his mother rule for him as he spent his days with wine and women. So to their shock the Chihalgani discovered that in spite of having kept Razia from becoming the sultan and having their own man on the throne, they were still being ruled by another woman.

Shah Turkan was very unpopular as she was a vengeful woman, generally preoccupied with intrigues and not too good at running the kingdom. She had another son of Iltutmish killed and when she started terrorising the other queens, the people of Delhi began to protest and even her own supporters left her. Soon another son of Iltutmish rebelled in Awadh and Firuz had to reluctantly march out of Delhi to face him.

Razia seized this opportunity. During the Friday prayers at the largest mosque she gave a passionate speech asking for justice and the people all rose to support her. She also had the support of the army who captured Shah Turkan and Razia was declared the sultan. When Firuz returned, he and Shah Turkan were put to death and Delhi had its one and only woman sultan.

Sultan Razia-al-din

We don't really know how old Razia was when she became the sultan but she was probably in her late twenties. The fact that she was a single woman at a time when girls were married in their teenage also makes her a very unusual woman.

Razia's first opposition came from her own chief minister, the vizier Nizamul Mulk Junaidi who clearly did not like the idea of a woman as his boss. Junaidi got some Turk noblemen to support him and declared war. Razia marched out at the head of her army and managed to create disunity among the rebels. As a result, many of the noblemen abandoned Junaidi. He fled from the battlefield and died soon after and some of the other rebel leaders were killed.

Razia returned to Delhi in triumph and as the Turk faction had supported Junaidi, she now appointed Tajiks in the high posts. A shrewd politician, she began to play one faction against another and in this way held on to power. Problems began when she appointed an Ethiopian called Malik Jamaluddin Yakut as Amir-i-Akhur—the master of the stables. It was a position of high prestige that was coveted by the Turks. Yakut became a close advisor and confidant and the other courtiers began to resent his rising influence with the sultan, especially the troublesome Turks.

Razia decided she was going to act like a real sultan. She began to appear in public wearing male attire, a short tunic, trousers and a conical hat and what shocked everyone was that she refused to veil her face. She sat on the throne in open court like her father and grandfather had done, listened to appeals, passed judgements and issued orders. Her subjects were very happy as she ran the government efficiently. She enjoyed meeting people and mingled among her subjects and the soldiers and was very popular with the citizens of Delhi.

In the brief time that she was sultan, Razia also devoted time to the welfare of her subjects. She established schools and libraries like the Nasiriya College that was headed by a scholar from Georgia named Al-Minhaj bin Siraj who wrote about the events of her reign. The common people supported her but the nobility had other ideas. They had thought they could control her because she was a woman but she was smart and independent. This made them resent her and pretty soon they were back to plotting rebellions against her.

The excuse for the next rebellion was Razia's friendship and trust for Jamaluddin Yakut. Razia and Yakut faced the rebel army and even killed some of them. Then a nobleman named Malik Altuniya who was the governor of Bhatinda managed to kill Yakut and captured Razia but things did not go the way Altuniya had planned. If he had expected to become the next sultan he was disappointed as the nobles put another son of Iltutmish named Muizuddin Bahram Shah on the throne. Probably to avoid being put to death, Razia agreed to marry Altuniya and then she cleverly incited Altuniya to gather an army and march to Delhi.

Razia and Altuniya were met by the forces of Bahram Shah and they were defeated. Soon after, their supporters deserted them and they began to flee from the Delhi army. In October 1240, Razia and Altuniya were both killed at Kaithal, Haryana by Jat robbers.

A good sultan

Razia may have ruled only for four years but within that short period she proved that she had all the qualities of a great leader. She was fearless on the battlefield, a shrewd politician and also a hardworking ruler who ran the kingdom with energy and efficiency. She had held the kingdom together but after her death decades of chaos followed as one weak ruler after another was put on the throne by the courtiers. The royal court was divided into various intriguing groups leading to an atmosphere of chaos and the ordinary people suffered.

Today we have prime ministers and presidents who are women. To understand Razia's achievement you have to remember that she lived 700 years ago. The state of women was very different in those times. Most of them were illiterate and had no rights to own property or live life their own way. The condition of women was not very good under Hindu rulers but with the arrival of the Muslims their freedom was even more curtailed. Now there was the system of compulsory purdah where women had to veil themselves and were forced to live in the women's quarters of the house. In the case of the rich this was the harem and these women were not allowed to meet any man outside the members of their own families. The Hindus also had the horrific tradition of sati where a wife burnt herself on the

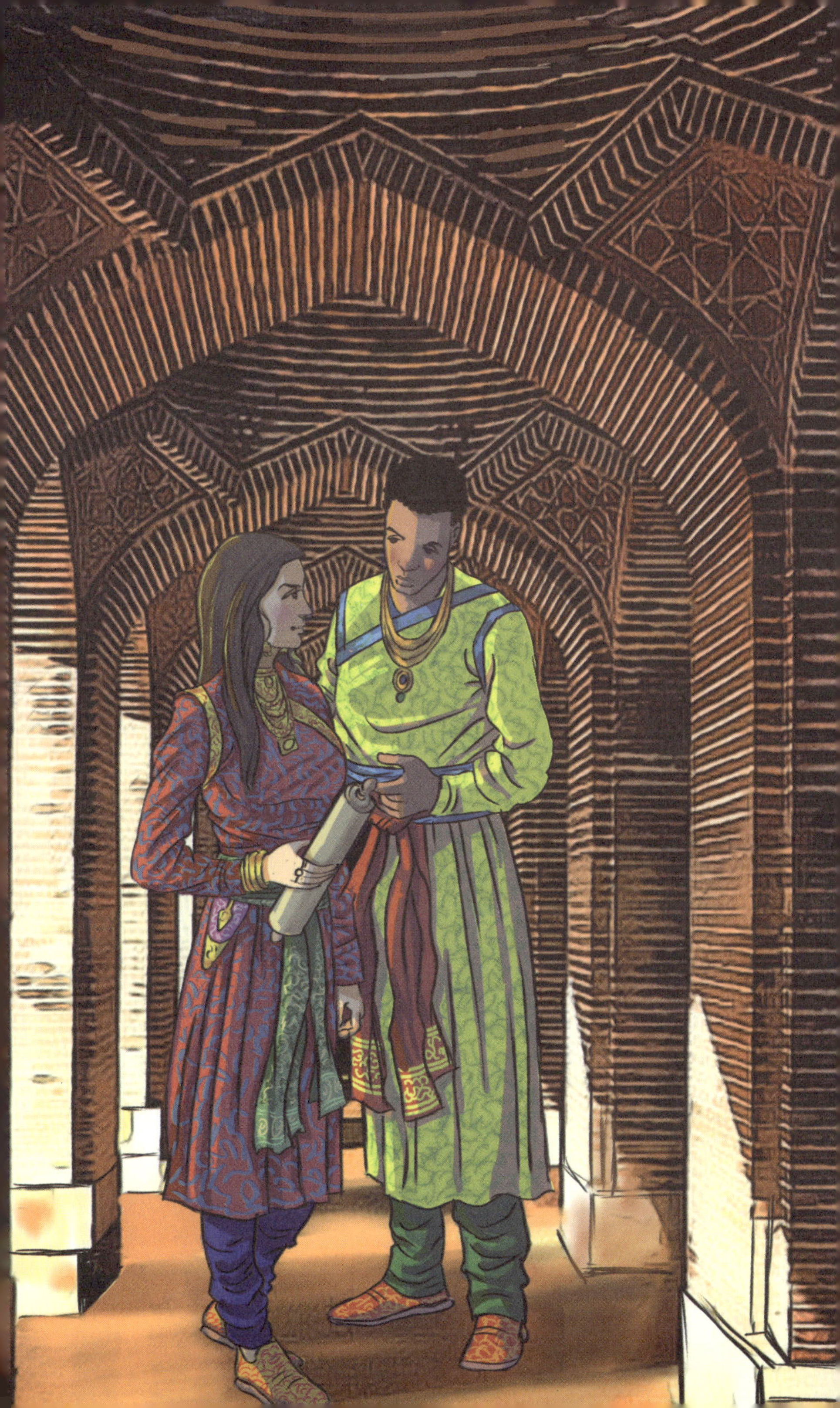

funeral pyre of her husband.

In such a society, Razia was intelligent, courageous and educated, learnt archery and riding, went hunting and led an army. She then ran the government in the absence of her father and fought to win and hold on to the throne. She fought for and gained her personal freedom by resisting being married off and locked up inside a harem. All this makes Razia a woman to be admired and remembered.

During India's history there were many queens who were the power behind the throne. They were often appointed as regents for their minor sons or as the wives of kings ruled from behind the purdah like the Mughal queen Nurjahan. Razia Sultan was the only true sultan who sat on the throne in her own right and it was because she had the courage to seize and hold on to power.

Sultans, Begums and Slaves

- Qutubuddin Aibak began building the Qutub Minar in Delhi that was completed by Iltutmish. The roofless tomb of Iltutmish stands nearby.
- The history of Razia Sultan can be found in the writings of the historian Al Minhaj bin Siraj who was her contemporary and the traveller Ibn Batuta who visited India a few years later during the reign of Muhammad bin Tughlak.
- In Delhi's Chandni Chowk there is a locality called Mohalla Bulbuli Khana. Here in an open courtyard surrounded by houses are two broken-down graves. Legends say these are the graves of Razia and her sister Shazia. As the graves bear no inscriptions, no one can be sure. Also in Razia's lifetime this area would have been a jungle as Chandni Chowk was built only in the seventeenth century.
- There were African courtiers in Delhi during the Sultanate. Jamaluddin Yakut is described as an (Abyssinian) or Ethiopian.
- Two other places, Kaithal, Haryana and Tonk in Rajasthan claim to have the tomb of Razia Sultan.
- Some historians of the time say Razia wanted to be called 'Sultan' and not 'Sultana' as a sultana is the wife of a sultan and she was a ruler in her own right.
- The kingdom of the Sultanate during the time of Iltutmish and Razia stretched from Lahore to Bengal.
- In 1983, director Kamal Amrohi made a film called *Razia Sultan* in which Hema Malini played Razia and Dharmendra in weird brown make-up played Jamaluddin Yakut.

- The American feminist writer Gloria Steinem includes the story of Razia in her book, *Herstory: Women Who Changed the World.*

Books You Can Read

1. *Medieval India* by Satish Chandra; Orient Blackswan
2. *The Wonder that was India* (vol II) by S.A.A. Rizvi; Picador
3. *Struggle for Empire* ed R.C. Majumdar; Bharatiya Vidya Bhawan
4. *Historic Delhi* by H.K. Kaul; Oxford University Press

KRISHNADEVA RAYA

(Reign 1509-1529 CE)

VIJAYANAGAR EMPIRE

- RAICHUR
- HAMPI
- ANANTAPUR
- PENUKONDA

ARABIAN SEA

BAY OF BENGAL

He is a king who deserves to be right there beside the most famous Indian emperors like Ashoka and Akbar but surprisingly very few Indians know about him. He shares so many qualities with the two kings who are given the title of 'Great' that it is surprising that he is not remembered with books and films about his reign. He was forgotten for centuries like the kingdom he ruled but Krishnadeva Raya, king of Vijayanagar is among the greatest monarchs India has seen.

Krishnadeva Raya of the Tuluva dynasty of Vijayanagar had much in common with the emperors Ashoka of the Maurya dynasty of Pataliputra and Akbar of the Mughal dynasty of Agra and Fatehpur Sikri. Not just as a successful warrior but also as an enlightened king.

Krishnadeva ruled over an empire that covered most of South India and he brought the Vijayanagar Empire to its zenith. He was a tough and enterprising army general who never lost a battle; he was a hard-working, wise and efficient ruler who understood the art of statecraft. He was also interested in architecture and encouraged trade, art and culture. He loved books and even wrote poetry. And most importantly, he shared a quality that truly marks a great king—a devotion to the welfare of his subjects and a genuine tolerance and acceptance of all religions.

If by some time-travelling magic Ashoka and Akbar could have met Krishnadeva Raya, they would have liked each other and have had much to talk about.

Vijayanagar? Where is it?

It was one of the greatest empires of South India that spanned from present day Andhra Pradesh to Kerala but if you look for any place called Vijayanagar in an atlas you won't find it. Today, the ruins of the city of Vijayanagar which was the capital of the empire, lie around a tiny village in Karnataka called Hampi. The nearest town is Hospet that you can reach by train or bus from Bangalore, then following a half hour ride by car or bus you are in Hampi.

The area has a fascinating landscape, with low hills and stretches of emerald paddy fields. It looks as if a mythical giant had danced around the hills making all these red gold boulders break off that now lie all around in tottering piles. Your car will go past sleepy villages with lengthy names and then the road starts climbing a low hill. When you reach the top, stop the car, get off and take in a breathtaking sight.

Right below, as far as the eyes can see, are the ruins of a legendary medieval city—granite palaces, temples, bazaars, gopuram gateways, pavilions and straggly stretches of city walls surrounded by the green of palm and areca trees. And through the ruins and the boulder-strewn hills flow the silver waters of the tumultuous Tungabhadra River. It is a landscape you never forget.

Devotees of the Ramayana say this is the site of the legendary Kishkindha where Ram and Lakshman met

Hanuman. Later, from the fourteenth to the sixteenth century travellers came from across the world and they called the city by many names—Pampakshetra, Virupakshapura, Kishkindhakshetra, Bidjanagar, Bisnaga, Vijayangar. Today the tourists just call it after a village named Hampi.

Two brave brothers

The beginning of Vijaynagar is like an adventure tale and the story starts in far-off Delhi in 1300 CE when Sultan Allauddin Khalji was on the throne. He was a man of bottomless greed. He had heard of the prosperous southern kingdoms and sent his general Malik Kafur on an expedition to plunder the temples and extract tribute from the Hindu kings. Kafur swept through the region, reached the southern tip of the peninsula at Rameswaram and returned to Delhi with a vast booty. Once Kafur left, the southern kingdoms rose again, and among them was the tiny kingdom of Kampili that stood by the Tungabhadra River. Its king, Kampiladeva, built the fort of Anegondi that you can still see at Hampi.

Allauddin Khalji had started a tradition of Delhi sultans sending their army south for plunder whenever they needed money. It was of course called a religious war or jihad but in fact it was just rooted in greed. The invasions became a familiar pattern—the sultan's army would march in, pillage, kill and withdraw and soon after the southern kingdoms

HAMPI

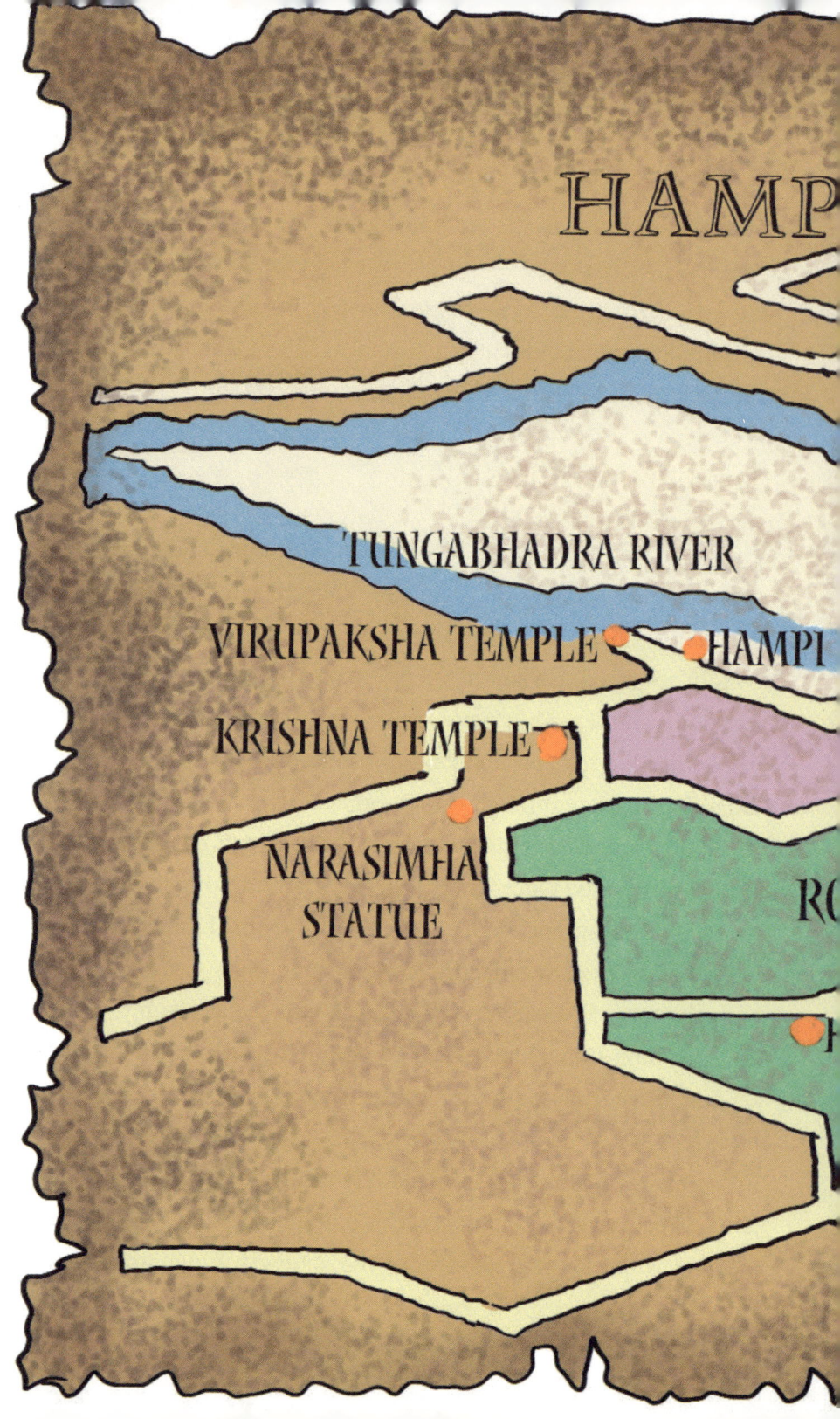

TUNGABHADRA RIVER

VIRUPAKSHA TEMPLE — HAMPI

KRISHNA TEMPLE

NARASIMHA STATUE

R...

MAP

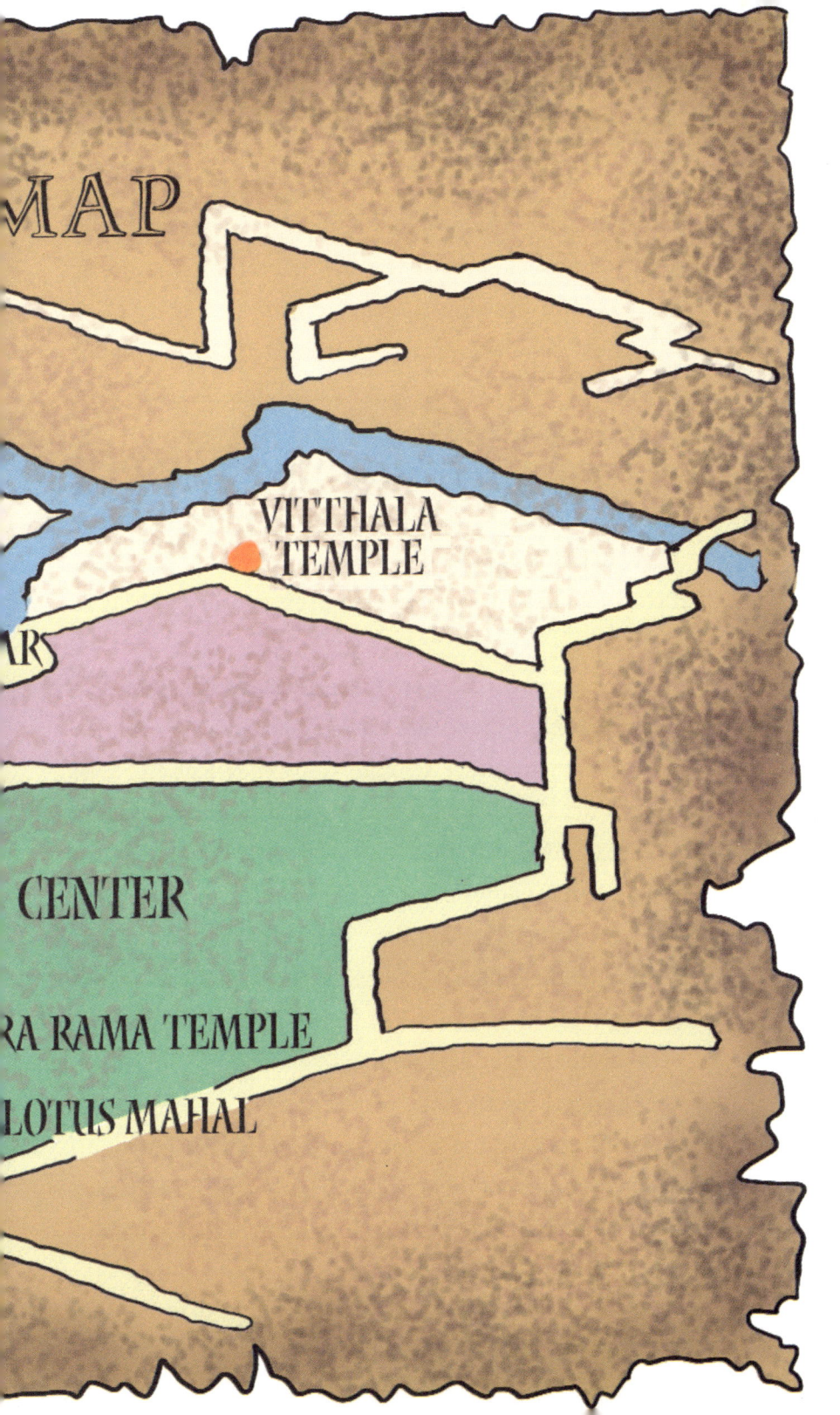

VITTHALA TEMPLE

CENTER

RA RAMA TEMPLE

LOTUS MAHAL

would rise again. The problem is that the kingdoms never thought of uniting against the invasions from the north. That was left to the kings of Vijayanagar.

The next sultanate army to arrive at the banks of the Tungabhadra was that of Muhammad bin Tughlak. The Tughlak army defeated Kampiladeva and captured the fort of Anegondi. After a tough fight, Kampiladeva was killed and among the prisoners of war were two brothers named Harihara and Bukka. The sons of a local chieftain named Sangama, the brothers had been treasury officers of Kampiladeva.

Harihara and Bukka were taken to Delhi and forced to convert to Islam. They were clever and enterprising men who knew how to please a sultan. Soon they won the trust of Muhammad bin Tughlak and became senior officials in the Tughlak administration. A few years later there was a rebellion at Kampili and the sultan decided to send them south as provincial governors. The brothers swore their allegiance to the sultan and headed south but luckily for our story, once in Kampili they changed their mind.

The brothers met a Hindu scholar named Vidyaranya of the Sringeri Peeth who inspired them to break free from Delhi and lay the foundation of a Hindu kingdom. Vidyaranya converted them back to Hinduism and Harihara and then Bukka ruled over a small independent kingdom that they called Vijayanagar and also at times Vidyanagar after their beloved guru. Then on the southern bank of the Tungabhadra they began to build a city that they called by the same name.

The kings of Vijayanagar were known as Raya, a form of the word raja. Harihara, Bukka and three of their brothers founded the Sangama dynasty that established Vijayanagar in 1336 CE. Two dynasties known as the Saluva and Tuluva would follow. Krishnadeva belonged to the latter. The empire of Vijayanagar at its zenith would include most of the Deccan and the southern peninsula and stretch across the modern states of Karnataka, Andhra Pradesh, Maharashtra, Tamil Nadu, Kerala and parts of Orissa. The Vijayanagar Empire would last for over two centuries, from 1336 to 1565 and its fame spread across Asia and Europe as travellers and merchants carried reports of a magnificent kingdom that was legendary for its riches, culture, architecture and elegant lifestyle.

Merely a prince

No one expected Krishnadeva to become the king. His half-brother Vira Narasimha was on the throne and it was assumed that his son would succeed as king. In 1509, when Vira Narasimha was dying, his son was still very young and so he instructed his chief minister Saluva Timma to blind Krishnadeva in order to stop him from taking the throne. As

Saluva felt that Krishnadeva was the right man for the throne, he did not obey and instead he made sure that Krishnadeva became the next king. The partnership of Krishnadeva and Saluva Timma would last for most of his reign.

When Krishnadeva came to the throne, the Vijayanagar Empire was surrounded by enemies waiting to attack. In the early years Vijayanagar had faced the enmity of the Gajapati kings of Orissa and the Bahmani kingdom of Gulbarga. Later, the Bahmani kingdom broke into five Muslim sultanates under five powerful governors—Bijapur, Golconda, Ahmednagar, Bidar and Berar and they looked with envy and greed at the riches of Vijayanagar and declared a religious war, a jihad.

Of the five sultanates, Bijapur was the most aggressive as it shared a border with Vijayanagar. In 1509, with a new and inexperienced king on the throne at Vijayanagar, Gajapati Prataparudra of Orissa, Sultan Mahmud of Gulbarga and Nawab Yusuf Adil Khan of Bijapur decided it was time to invade and collect some booty.

So within a few months of his coronation, Krishnadeva had to fight the army of the Bahmani sultan Mahmud. The sultan faced a crushing defeat by the Vijayanagar forces, not once but twice. Then Yusuf Khan marched in from Bijapur and was killed at the Battle of Kovelakonda. With their sultan dead, years of internal turmoil followed in Bijapur and Vijayanagar was left in peace for some time.

Krishnadeva then made sure his enemies got the message as his army swept into the kingdoms of his enemies. He first entered Gulbarga, the capital of the Bahmanis, followed by the capture of the fort of Bidar and then while withdrawing he allowed Mahmud to return to the throne.

With Bijapur and the Bahmanis defeated, Krishnadeva came back to a huge welcome at Vijayanagar and assumed a new title—Yavana-rajya-sthapan-acharya, the lord who had established a kingdom in the land of the heathens. The message was clear, you mess with Vijayanagar only at your own peril.

Krishnadeva vs Prataparudra

During the rule of earlier kings, Prataparudra, the Gajapati of Orissa had captured two provinces from Vijayanagar—Udayagiri and Kondavidu. In 1513, Krishnadeva decided it was time to recover them. This campaign went on to prove his military genius. The moment Prataparudra heard that the Vijayanagar army was approaching, he sent a large force to protect the Udayagiri fort. Krishnadeva first met this army, defeated them, pushed them out and then tackled the challenge of laying siege of the fort.

A siege of the fortress of Udayagiri was going to be a challenge. The fort was situated on a hill. There was only one road going up to it and it was so narrow that only one man could go up at a time. So an attacking army had to climb up in a single file while facing the enemy archers, cannons and rocks. Krishnadeva first had the road widened, then all the other exits from the fort were blocked by walls and finally the army began to move up. Seeing rows and rows of soldiers marching up the hill the Orissa garrison panicked and promptly surrendered.

The next target was Kondavidu where Saluva Timma met with a tough fight till Krishnadeva devised a new way to capture a fort. Tall wooden platforms called nadachapparam were built and dragged to the walls of the fort and as the garrison watched in surprise the soldiers clambered up and jumped over the walls. Prataparudra moved quickly to attack the Vijayangar forces from behind and Krishnadeva promptly turned his army around to face this new threat. Even though they were attacked while crossing a river, Vijayanagar triumphed again. The Oriya army withdrew and the Kondavidu fort and province were captured.

As Krishnadeva toured the province in triumph, the Oriya general Shitab Khan planned a retaliation. Krishnadeva's spies informed him that Shitab Khan had positioned 6,000 archers across a narrow mountain pass and they were waiting to ambush the Vijayanagar forces. Instead of a face-to-face encounter, Krishnadeva chose a clever stratagem. He ordered his horsemen to climb the hills and attack the waiting Oriya archers from behind till they were routed and fled in panic. Then as the Vijayanagar forces captured Prataparudra's capital Cuttack, finally the Gajapati sued for peace.

Bijapur moves again

Surrounded by enemy kingdoms, Vijayanagar and Krishnadeva Raya were not allowed to live in peace. Soon after his triumph over Orissa, the combined forces of Golconda under Quli Qutub Shah and Bijapur led by Ismail Adil Khan led a two-pronged attack. The Vijayanagar forces had to be divided between Saluva Timma and Krishnadeva. Timma defeated Golconda and the king dealt such a crushing blow on Bijapur that the sultan fled leaving his cannons and army camp behind him. Then Krishnadeva moved on to capture the strategically important Raichur fortress. During the siege he was helped by Portuguese musketeers led by the Portuguese general Christovao de Figueiredo.

Vijayanagar held a yearly Mahanavami festival in autumn and during the next one that was a celebration of the king's victories, Figueiredo was gifted a robe by Krishnadeva. Another Portuguese in the contingent was a trader named Domingo Paes who has left us a detailed description of the magnificent celebrations comprising of marching soldiers, elephants, horses and dancing girls.

With these convincing victories over Orissa, Golconda and Bijapur, Krishnadeva finally established a period of peace. In the last decade of his reign, he watched Vijayanagar flourish as the richest kingdom in the land. Travellers and traders flocked to its legendary bazaars from many countries like the Portuguese Domingo Paes and Fernao Nuniz; the Italians Nicolo dei Conti and Ludovico di Varthema; the Persian Abdur Razzaq and the Russian Athanasius Nikitin. They have all left accounts of their travels and the portrait of Vijayanagar emerges as a prosperous and peaceful city inhabited by people who were cared for and devoted to their king.

The Warrior-King

Krishnadeva shared many characteristics with the Mughal king Akbar. Like Akbar, he never lost a battle. He was also a hard-working king who ran an efficient administration and was always conscious of his duty to care for his subjects, making sure they were treated with generosity and justice. For both these enlightened monarchs, a person's abilities mattered, not his religion and so just as Akbar had Hindu courtiers and officials, Krishnadeva had Muslim soldiers and generals and these soldiers took their oath of loyalty on the Quran. The traveller Barbosa writes, 'The king allows such freedom that every man may come and go and live according to his own creed, without suffering any annoyance.'

As a general, Krishnadeva led his army from the front and he inspired his men by his clever military strategy and courage. He often won a battle like the siege of Udayagiri by devising a new plan and his royal flag bearing the image of a boar flew over the capitals of all his enemies—Bijapur, Gulbarga, Cuttack and Bidar. Even though he occupied these places Krishnadeva never looted any city or massacred the people. Unlike the Muslim forces that completely devastated Vijayanagar once they occupied it, Krishnadeva won the loyalty of his soldiers by taking a personal interest in their welfare. After every battle he would wander around searching for the wounded and he would reward the good fighters. He also knew the value of horses and muskets in warfare and with this aim in mind he allied with the Portuguese rulers of Goa.

We are all familiar with the tall gateways of the temples of the south called gopurams. The first gopuram was built for the Virupaksha Temple at Vijayanagar by Krishnadeva. Some of the finest temples here were built by him like the Vitthala and Krishna temples. The giant granite image of Narasimha that stands guard over the city with such ferocious pride, was carved during his reign.

The ruins of the temples, bazaars and palaces still give us an idea of the prosperity of Vijayangar. Travellers

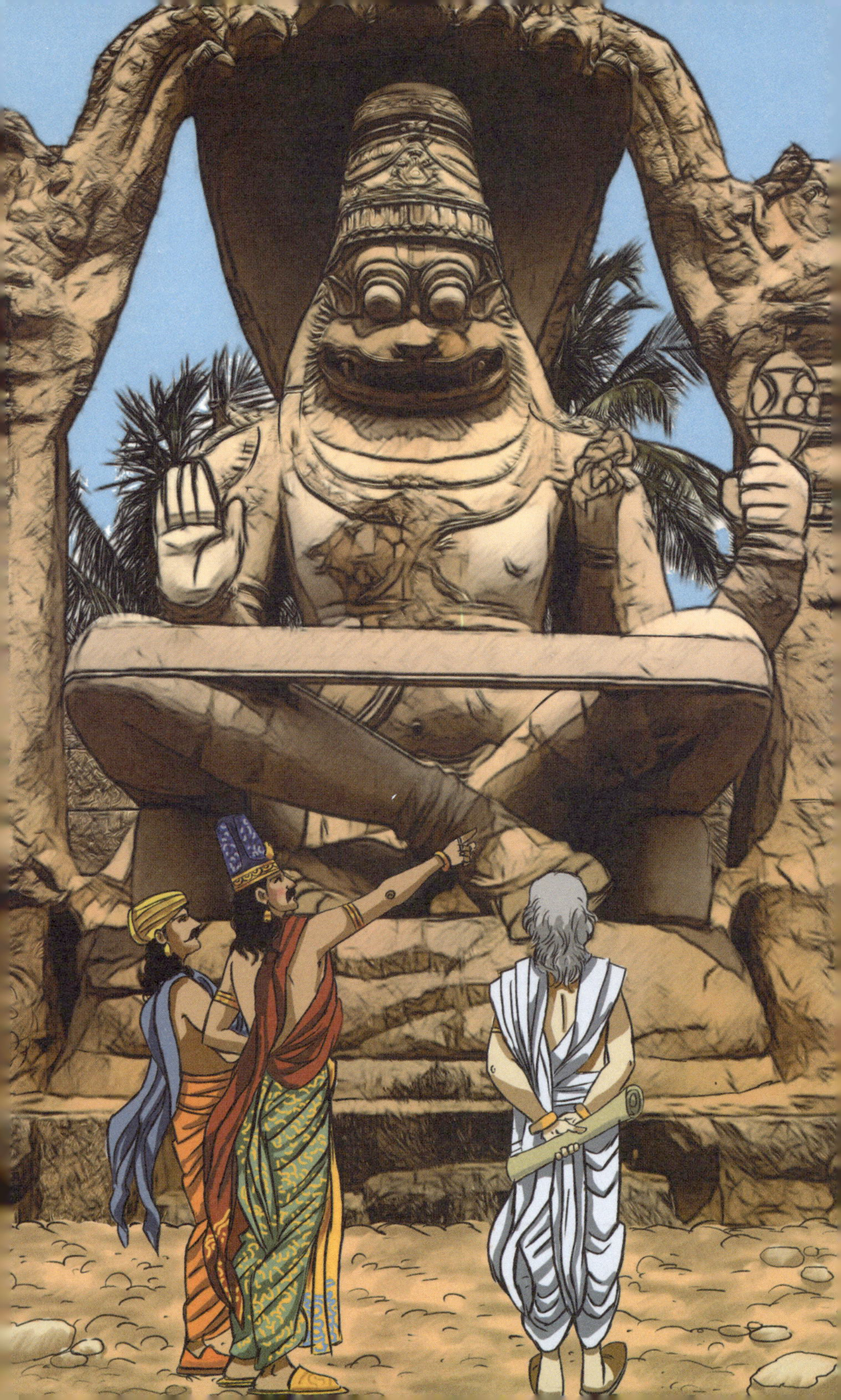

describe palaces filled with gold, silver, gems and silks. The Mahanavami festival saw magnificent processions that dazzled the visitors. Even the elephants and horses were caparisoned with silks and precious metal. As Varthema says about Krishnadeva's stables, 'His horse is worth more than some of our cities, on account of the ornaments which he wears.' Paes writes that the royal ladies were so laden with jewellery that they needed maids to help them walk!

Krishnadeva worked tirelessly for his kingdom. When he was not at war to defend it, he was on tour meeting his people. On these royal journeys he listened to the complaints of his subjects and accepted their petitions. This meant that the local officials had to do their job properly or the wrath of the king would be upon them. As this region does not get a lot of rainfall, much was done to improve agriculture with the digging of irrigation channels and water reservoirs. Craftspeople and traders were encouraged so that the bazaars of the city became famous across the world with merchants from Portugal to China wandering around the glittering shops looking for cotton and silk textiles, jewellery and spices.

Tenali and others

There was one man in Krishnadeva Raya's court who we still remember—a poet and humourist named Tenali

Ramakrishna Kavi or, as we know him, Tenali Raman. Like Raja Birbal in Akbar's court, Tenali Raman was a popular poet who is remembered more for his wit. Krishnadeva was a great patron and his court was made up of many talented men like him.

The king was himself a poet and one of his long verses, *Amukta Malyada*, has survived. In this poem he describes the duties of a king. The work has been praised by scholars for its poetic qualities. He was proud to be a patron of arts and letters and in his court there were eight writers of Sanskrit, Telugu and Kannada who were honoured with the title of Ashtadiggajas, the eight great scholars. The most revered was the poet Allasani Pedanna, who was made poet laureate by the king and at the initiation ceremony Krishnadeva himself tied a gold anklet on his leg and then lifted Pedanna's palanquin onto his shoulders.

Domingo Paes on Krishnadeva

The only portraits we have of Krishnadeva are stone and metal images but we are very lucky to get a description of his character from a man who saw him up close—Domingo Paes, a man who was very impressed by the king.

Paes writes about this many hued monarch, 'The king is of medium height and of fair complexion and good figure, rather fat than thin; he has on his face signs of small pox.

He was the most feared and perfect king that could possibly be, cheerful of disposition and very merry; he is one that seeks to honour foreigners and receives them kindly asking about all their affairs whatever their conditions may be. He is a great ruler and a man of much justice, but subject to sudden fits of rage.'

As a great warrior, Krishnadeva was an energetic and athletic man and Paes says, 'The king is accustomed everyday to drink a quartilho of oil of gingelly, and anoint himself all over with the said oil; he covers his loins with a small cloth, and takes in his arms great weights made of earthenware and then, taking a sword, he exercises himself with it till he has sweated out all the oil, and then he wrestles with one of his wrestlers. After this labour he mounts a horse and gallops about the plain in one direction and another till dawn, for he does all this before day break.'

The last days

Through all his triumphs there was a personal sadness in Krishnadeva's life. He had no living son. Then in 1518, Queen Tirumale gave birth to a son who was named Tirumale Deva. In 1524, when the boy was about six years old, Krishnadeva decided to crown him king and become the regent who would rule for him till the boy came of age. However, to his utter sorrow the boy died a few months later.

Soon rumours began to fly about and the king was told that Saluva Timma's son Timma Dandanayaka had poisoned Tirumale Deva. A grief-stricken Krishnadeva believed the news. Saluva Timma and his two sons were imprisoned and blinded and the old minister died soon after. It was a huge blow to Krishnadeva who was so close to Saluva Timma he called him 'appaji' or father. After Saluva helped him win the throne he had been the king's trusted adviser as well as a powerful general. Historians think that even if Dandanayaka was guilty, Saluva Timma was innocent but Krishnadeva in his grief did not believe it.

Krishnadeva was still in his forties when he fell ill and died in 1529. His younger brother Achyuta Raya became king and ascended the diamond throne of Vijayanagar. Unfortunately, after Krishnadeva the kings of Vijayanagar were weak men and there was so much intrigue in the royal family that courtiers and local governors often rose in rebellion. Realizing this weakness the combined forces of the five Sultanate kingdoms attacked in 1565 and Vijayanagar was defeated at the Battle of Talikota. The city was looted; the buildings smashed and burnt to the ground; the people fled and Vijayanagar never rose again.

For centuries Vijayanagar, the last great Hindu empire, remained forgotten and soon the ruins of the city were swallowed up by nature. Trees and grass grew around the carved pillars, farmers planted paddy along the bazaars and wild animals roamed by the temples. The only living spaces that remained were the Virupaksha Temple and a small village called Hampi.

The spirit of Krishnadeva Raya still lives on in the soaring gopuram gateway that he built for the Virupaksha Temple, the pavilions of the Hampi Bazaar and in the courtyards of the deserted Krishna and Vitthala temples where tourists wander about looking in amazement at the exquisitely-carved pillars, ceilings and walls carved with friezes of dancing girls, horses and elephants, mythical monsters and deities. Even today, Vijayanagar-Hampi is Krishnadeva Raya's magnificent city.

A Vijayanagar Vignette

- The Virupaksha Temple that stands at one end of Hampi Bazaar is older than the Vijayanagar Empire. The kings of Vijayanagar proclaimed that the real monarch of their kingdom was Lord Virupaksha and his consort Pampa Devi, their family deities. Virupaksha is another name for Lord Shiva and Pampa is the goddess Parvati.
- The coronations of the kings of Vijayanagar were held in the Virupaksha Temple and all the royal papers were signed in the god's name.
- The temple of Acharya Vidyaranya, who inspired Harihar and Bukka to build a Hindu kingdom, still stands on Matanga Hill beside the Virupaksha temple.
- There is a romantic story of a young Krishnadeva when he was still a prince. He fell in love with a courtesan and she jokingly asked him if he would make her a queen if he became king. He kept his promise and married her when he won the throne.
- Women lived and moved about freely in Vijayangar and there was no purdah. Many women worked in the royal palaces as officials and there are mentions of female accountants and wrestlers!
- Vijayanagar was forgotten till the twentieth century when Robert Sewell wrote the book *A Forgotten Empire*.
- The first European colony in India was the Portuguese colony of Goa and Vijayanagar bought Arab horses from them. Portuguese soldiers fought in the Vijayanagar army, especially as musketeers. Today the road connecting Goa

- to Hampi still exists.
- The foreign travellers had a lot of problem spelling the Telugu and Kannada names. Vijayanagar was spelled as Bisnaga, Bichenagar, Bidjanagar, Bisnagar, Bizemegalia, Visajanagar and Beejanagar. Some refer to it as the 'Kingdom of Narsymga' meaning the Narasimha image.
- During the reign of Allauddin Khalji the booty of his general Malik Kafur from the south was reported to be 612 elephants, 20,000 horses, boxes of precious gems and pearls and 96,000 maunds of gold. Considering that one maund is 68 kilos, it has to be an exaggeration.
- Krishnadeva visited the Venkateshwara temple at Tirupati thrice and his gifts included a jewel-studded crown, a pearl necklace, silver plates, a sword decorated with diamonds, rubies and sapphires and 30,000 gold coins that were poured over the god. The offerings must have covered the image.

Books You Can Read

A Forgotten Empire by Robert Sewell; Asian Educational Services

Vijayanagar by Burton Stein; Cambridge University Press

Monumental Legacy, Hampi by Anila Verghese; Oxford University Press

Hampi Ruins by A.H. Longhurst; Asian Educational Services

Hampi by J.M. Fritz and G. Mitchell; India Book House

NURJAHAN

(Reign 1611-1627 CE)

MUGHAL EMPIRE

- KABUL
- PESHAWAR
- GHAZNI
- KANDAHAR
- LAHORE
- PANIPAT
- DELHI
- FATEHPUR SIKRI
- AGRA
- LUCKNOW
- PATNA
- PLASSEY

DECCAN

There has only been one empress in the Mughal dynasty. She was an extraordinary woman who ruled the empire, built monuments and had coins minted in her name. Nurjahan began as a minor queen, the last and youngest of the many wives of Emperor Jahangir but through sheer willpower, personality, courage and political skill, she gradually became the centre of power.

What makes Nurjahan so remarkable was that she could wield such authority and influence from behind the purdah of the royal harem. Many Mughal women had been powerful like Akbar's mother Hamida Banu, his aunt Gulbadan Begum and wife Salima Sultan but their influence over the king was because they had won the love and trust of the king and they acted as his advisers. Nurjahan was different. She was in fact the person who ran the empire and took decisions about state matters in the name of the king.

Jahangir gave her the title Nurjahan, 'light of the world' and she continues to fascinate historians and writers even today.

A girl called Mihrunnisa

She was born Mihrunnisa, 'sun among women' to a Persian nobleman Mirza Ghiyas Beg and his wife Asmat Begum. In Persia, the family had fallen on bad times and Ghiyas Beg decided to travel to India hoping to find work in the court of the Mughal emperor Akbar. During their journey from Persia to India, Mihrunnisa was born in 1577 at Kandahar in Afghanistan. One story says that her parents were in desperate straits as they had been robbed of all their possessions and they abandoned the infant on the wayside. The baby was saved by the leader of the caravan, who took pity on Ghiyas Beg and once they reached India he introduced Beg to Akbar at Fatehpur Sikri.

At that time, the Mughal Empire was the richest in the world and the court of Akbar saw the arrival of talented men from all across the Muslim world seeking work. Soon Ghiyas Beg had won the approval of the emperor by his hard work and scholarship. He was a very efficient bureaucrat and known for his generosity but was also notorious for being a highly corrupt man. The historian Muhammad Hadi writes about this supreme Mughal courtier, 'Mirza Ghiyas Beg was so charitably disposed that no one ever left his door dissatisfied; but in the taking of bribes he certainly was most uncompromising and fearless.'

Ghiyas Beg's rise in the Mughal bureaucracy was a smooth one. After the death of Akbar in 1605, his son Salim became king and took the title of Jahangir, 'ruler of the world'. Ghiyas Beg was appointed the revenue minister by Jahangir and given the title of Itimad-ud-daula, 'pillar of the government'. To be called the pillar, he must have been really good at his job. Jahangir even praised him in his autobiography *Tuzuk-i-Jahangiri*, writing, 'He showed loyalty to the sovereign, and yet left pleased and hopeful him who was in need.' So Mihrunnisa grew up in an affluent household where state matters were frequently discussed and she was familiar with the nobility and the politics within the royal family.

Enter Sher Afgan

When Mihrunnisa was seventeen, she was married to a Persian nobleman named Ali Quli Beg Istajlu, popularly called Sher Afgan, 'tiger slayer', because he was said to have fought a tiger barehanded. Jahangir had posted him to Bengal as a landlord with a jagir in Burdwan and Mihrunnisa followed her husband there.

Sher Afgan was a brave soldier but a man of reckless ambitions. At that time, Jahangir's eldest son Khusrau was rebelling against his father and the governor of Bengal Qutubuddin Khan suspected that Sher Afgan was supporting Khusrau. In 1607, when the governor arrived at Burdwan to investigate, Sher Afgan suddenly attacked and killed the unsuspecting man but was himself then slain by the governor's guards. Later when Jahangir married Mihrunissa there were rumours that he had got Sher Afgan killed but that does not really make sense. If the Mughal emperor wanted to marry the wife of any nobleman, the courtly

COINS

tradition was that the husband would divorce her and she would then enter the royal harem. If he wanted to marry Mihrunissa, all Jahangir had to do was ask, very politely of course!

The widowed Mihrunnisa now returned to Agra with her daughter Ladli Begum and was appointed as the lady in waiting to Ruqaiyya Begum, one of the widows of Akbar. She worked quietly in the royal harem for four years before she caught the eye of Jahangir at a harem bazaar. This festival was called Meena Bazaar and had been started by Akbar. It took place on the Persian New Year of Navroz. The ladies of the harem set up shops where the men of the royal family came to buy their goods. The ladies sold at exorbitant prices of course and there was a lot of good-natured bargaining. It was a great way to flirt with the ladies. Here, Jahangir met Mihrunnisa and was captivated by her beauty, quick wit and charm.

Jahangir's youngest wife

In 1611, Jahangir married Mihrunissa. By then he was

a much-married man with no one being really sure of the number of queens and concubines. The number was probably around twenty-five queens and 200 concubines! What is remarkable is that after Mihrunissa he did not marry again, even though they did not have any children. At the time of marriage Jahangir was forty-two and Mihrunnisa was thirty-four. Surprisingly, it became a marriage of love and respect where she succeeded in becoming his constant companion and greatest support.

Legends say she was very beautiful and she must have been a woman with a vibrant personality. Jahangir first gave her the title of Nur Mahal, 'light of the palace' and then promoted her to Nurjahan, 'light of the world'. Then on the death of Jahangir's mother Mariam-us-zamani he appointed her as the head of the harem with the title of Padshah Begum. With a harem of thousands of women this was a position of power and responsibility. She became Padshah Begum in spite of being his youngest queen.

Usually portraits of the royal women

PERFUME BOTTLE AND TRAY

were made by the male artists of the royal miniature studios from sketches made by women artists who had access to the harem. However, Jahangir was a connoisseur of paintings and must have supervised her portraits so they probably show her real face. In the portraits that have survived we see a woman with a broad forehead, large eyes under curving brows, a sharp aquiline nose and a small pouting mouth. In some of the paintings she is seen holding a wine cup with a slight smile curving her lips. Clearly she enjoyed her wine.

Contemporary historians describe her as a woman of many talents. She was an artist who designed carpets, jewellery and legends say she invented the shadow work chikan embroidery that is still done in Lucknow. She was highly educated, wrote poetry and was interested in politics and economics. She was also generous in helping the poor. She is said to have paid the dowry of thousands of orphaned girls. She was also a lively conversationalist and enjoyed throwing magnificent parties for the royal family. She helped Jahangir design the gardens of Srinagar in Kashmir and built a jewel-like mausoleum for her father Itimad-ud-daula in Agra.

The Empress and her clique

As he grew older Jahangir became less and less interested in the work of running the empire. Since he was a boy, he

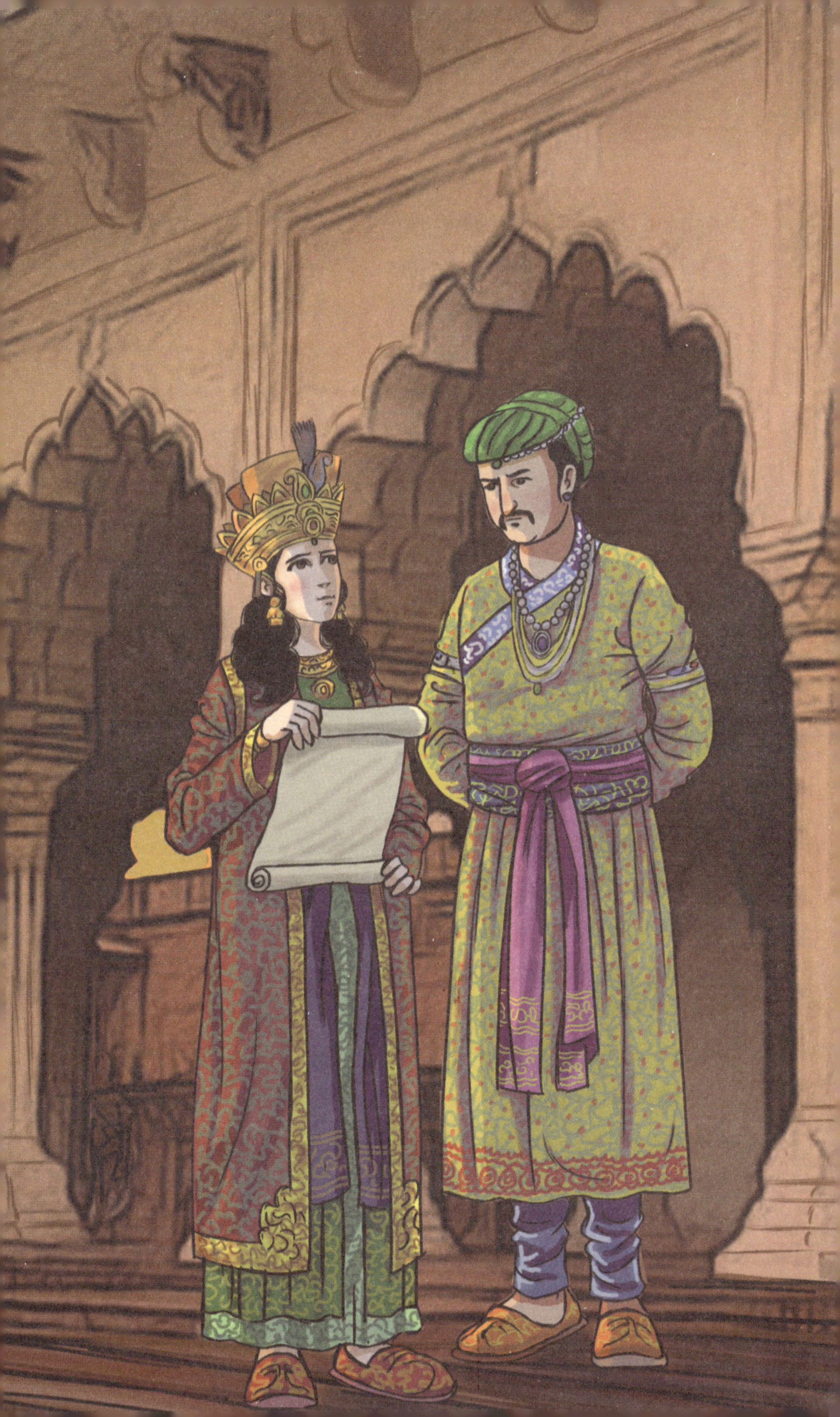

had been addicted to wine and opium and often fell ill. Nurjahan was his most trusted wife and gradually she took over the day to day running of the government. However, she had a problem, she was a woman who could not move out of the harem, sit in court or meet officials like any king would do. So she turned for help to her family and her biggest support came from her father Ghiyas Beg and her older brother Asaf Khan who were both senior courtiers.

The last member of the clique that worked with Nurjahan was Jahangir's third son Khurram. He was the most talented of the princes, a favourite of Akbar, a great warrior and general and an efficient administrator. What made this alliance even stronger was that one year after Nurjahan's marriage, Khurram married Arjamand Banu, Asaf Khan's daughter and Nurjahan's niece. One day, Khurram would take the throne as Shahjahan and Arjamand would be given the title of Mumtaz Mahal.

A few years later Ghiyas Beg died and Khurram following a disagreement with his father, marched off to Mandu and started a rebellion. One of the reasons behind Khurram's anger was a power struggle between him and Nurjahan. The trouble started when she married her daughter Ladli Begum to the youngest son of Jahangir called Shahriyar who was a feckless young prince. Jahangir was becoming sicker by the day and Khurram now feared that Nurjahan was plotting to put Shahriyar on the throne at his father's death and thus continue to run the empire.

While Khurram was wandering around Central India sporadically attacking the royal forces, Nurjahan and Asaf Khan continued running the empire for the last five years of Jahangir's reign. Jahangir who was often unwell did nothing without consulting them. Nurjahan read and wrote the royal orders called firmans and we still have some that were signed by her beside the signature of Jahangir. She approved all official promotions and issued grants. She even met officers while sitting behind a carved stone screen called jharokha, questioned them and gave orders and met her subjects and listened to their petitions. Nurjahan proved that a woman could rule an empire in spite of being hidden behind the purdah.

This rise of the family of Ghiyas Beg of course made the other courtiers very unhappy and among them was a general called Mahabat Khan who was a trusted friend of Jahangir from his youth. Mahabat Khan begged Jahangir to curb the powers of Nurjahan but Jahangir

FIRMAN

did not listen. The king had discovered that his wife was a superb administrator who kept an eye on every government department and he was happy with her taking care of all the work.

Jahangir suffered from asthma and disliked the heat and dust of Agra and so every summer Nurjahan would take him to Kashmir. Here she created the beautiful Shalimar Bagh, a garden with rows of fountains, water channels and marble pavilions set among landscaped flower beds. It was a place where Jahangir would relax.

Mahabat Khan rebels

Meanwhile, the power struggle within the royal family continued and now began to get really ugly. Jahangir had four sons and his eldest son Khusrau who had been blinded for rebelling against his father was dead. Khusrau was in the custody of Khurram and had probably been poisoned at Khurram's orders. Now the battle for the throne was between the three princes Parviz, Khurram and Shahriyar.

The prince next in line was Parviz while the third son Khurram had rebelled and been defeated by the royal army led by the general Mahabat Khan. He was at that time sulking in Central India. Mahabat Khan's success made Nurjahan very nervous as he supported Parviz while Asaf Khan preferred his son-in-law Khurram and Nurjahan was in favour of Shahriyar. So Nurjahan promptly had Mahabat Khan transferred to Bengal and Parviz was sent off to the other end of the empire as governor of Gujarat.

Then Mahabat Khan made a mistake of protocol. The tradition in the royal court was that when a nobleman arranged the marriage of his children he had to take the permission of the king. In 1626, Mahabat had his daughter engaged to a soldier without informing Jahangir. The king was furious. At that time Jahangir and Nurjahan were travelling from Lahore to Kabul and Mahabat Khan was summoned to meet the king. The royal camp had been set up by the banks of the Jhelum River where Mahabat Khan arrived with a contingent of 5,000 Rajput soldiers planning to explain his conduct and beg for the king's pardon.

No one felt threatened by the presence of Mahabat Khan and on that day most of the royal camp—soldiers, servants, Asaf Khan and Nurjahan herself, had crossed over to the other side of the river. When Mahabat Khan realized that Jahangir was being guarded very lightly he ordered his soldiers to destroy the boat bridge across the river to prevent the army from marching back. He then entered the royal tent with a band of soldiers and surrounded Jahangir. Mahabat Khan probably had not planned to capture the king and only acted impulsively when he saw an opportunity to have Jahangir within his power without the presence of Nurjahan.

A general kidnapping the king was such an unimaginable act that the guards were unprepared for Mahabat charging into the royal tent. A courtier named Mutamid Khan who was present there writes that when Jahangir came out Mahabat addressed him courteously and requested that the king should ride out in procession on his elephant so that people should not suspect anything was wrong. Shahriyar was also in the royal camp but he was too scared to defy Mahabat Khan.

Across the river, Nurjahan realized something was wrong and ordered the noblemen to lead an attack to rescue the king but the operation failed. Nurjahan herself led the troops on an elephant and aimed arrows at the enemy from the covered howdah. One of the first to flee was Asaf Khan but Nurjahan courageously decided to cross back and join her husband. Soon Asaf Khan also returned and joined his sister in captivity. The king, queen and their chief minister had no option but to obey and do what Mahabat Khan ordered. Oddly, Mahabat behaved very indecisively. He had kidnapped the king on an impulse with no plan in mind and allowed the royal entourage to go on to Kabul as planned.

Outwardly everything looked normal as Jahangir entered Kabul in procession, sitting on his elephant, scattering coins to the people. In public, Mahabat Khan was courteous to the king and his wife but in reality they were prisoners who acted as if they were reconciled to their fate. What Nurjahan realized was that the old general did not really know what to do next and she started plotting a rescue. The other noblemen in the royal entourage were full of envy at Mahabat's new power and she gathered them into a group to oppose him. She secretly sent out money to the chieftains of nearby fortresses and began to put together a new army. Meanwhile Jahangir acted as if he was happy with the new situation and obeyed Mahabat's requests.

In November 1626, when they were on their way back from Kabul, Jahangir asked Mahabat Khan to ride ahead with his soldiers and said he would like to review Nurjahan's troops. Realizing that a new army was ready to fight him, Mahabat Khan panicked and took flight but managed to take Asaf Khan and his son Shaista Khan as hostages. This was a mistake as now Jahangir and Nurjahan were surrounded by loyal troops and the empress sent a message ordering Mahabat Khan to release the hostages. Finally losing his nerve Mahabat let go of Asaf Khan and his son and went marching away into the wilderness. Nurjahan had won.

Jahangir's last days

Meanwhile news of Mahabat Khan's actions had reached Khurram and he began marching towards Lahore supposedly to rescue his father. The fleeing Mahabat Khan met him on the way and joined him. They could not do much because now Nurjahan and Jahangir had the royal troops and the king's personal ahadi guards around them. Khurram decided to bide his time as he knew that his father-in-law Asaf Khan was secretly on his side.

Jahangir's health was failing rapidly and the royal couple decided to go to Kashmir where they spent the summer of 1627. In autumn, when the royal camp began to travel towards Lahore, Jahangir became very ill and he died on the way on 7 November 1627 at the age of fifty-eight.

For Nurjahan, her power came from the king and now she also lost the support of her brother Asaf Khan. She wanted her son-in-law Shahriyar to become king while Asaf Khan wanted his son-in-law Khurram on the throne. The problem was that she was not popular among the courtiers and no one took Shahriyar seriously while Khurram was the most able prince and enjoyed the support of the nobility.

Asaf Khan sent a fast runner to Khurram with the news of Jahangir's death and he began to march towards Lahore. Then Asaf Khan put a guard around Nurjahan's tent and she was not able to reach Shahriyar who was in Lahore. By this time Jahangir's second son Parviz was dead and a son of Khusrau called Dawar Baksh was placed on the throne as a temporary king. Asaf Khan and Dawar Baksh then defeated and captured Shahriyar.

At Khurram's orders all the rival princes were put to

death by Asaf Khan including the feckless Shahriyar and the poor deluded Dawar Baksh. Khurram arrived at Lahore and was declared king. Assuming the title of Shahjahan he soon moved to Agra. Asaf Khan was made the vakil or chief minister and his daughter Arjamand was now the empress Mumtaz Mahal. With her brother, niece and Khurram ranged against her, Nurjahan lost this final battle.

Nurjahan being a very intelligent woman now withdrew gracefully and decided to retire and live in Lahore. Shahjahan was generous and gave her an annual allowance of two lakh rupees. Both she and her daughter Ladli Begum had been widowed within weeks of each other and they remained in Lahore where Nurjahan busied herself supervising the building of the mausoleum of Jahangir. Nurjahan died on 18 November 1645 having survived Jahangir by eighteen years. No one knows how long Ladli Begum lived.

Nurjahan had also built her own tomb in Lahore near Jahangir's mausoleum where the graves of the mother and daughter stand beside each other.

A MUGHAL MASALA

- The tombs of Nurjahan's first husband Sher Afgan and Qutubuddin, the man he murdered, lie next to each other in Burdwan, West Bengal.
- Nurjahan enjoyed hunting from behind a curtained howdah. She was a sharp shot with a musket and once shot four tigers with six bullets.
- Jahangir wrote his autobiography titled *Tuzuk-i-Jahangiri* where Nurjahan is mentioned often. However he does not talk about his marriage to her, probably because at that time it was not important. She became powerful later.
- Nurjahan was famous for her parties, which served a delicious cuisine and offered many kinds of entertainment like fireworks and dancers.
- Ghiyas Beg's family rose high—his daughter Nurjahan and granddaughter Mumtaz Mahal became queens. Beg, his son Asaf Khan and grandson Shaista Khan were senior ministers.
- Ghiyas Beg, Itimad-ud-daula was so completely trusted by Jahangir that he was allowed to enter the royal harem and the ladies did not veil themselves before him.
- Nurjahan's mother Asmat Begum invented the perfume attar of roses and Jahangir gifted her with a pearl necklace for her creation.
- In Lahore the tomb of Asaf Khan stands between the tombs of Jahangir and Nurjahan.
- Nurjahan issued a set of twelve gold coins with the symbols

of the zodiac signs on them and her name stamped on the back.
- Many of the harem ladies owned ships that traded with the Middle East, Africa and Europe taking spices, textiles and indigo. The two smartest businesswomen were Jahangir's mother Mariam-us-zamani and his wife Nurjahan.
- On his way to the throne Shahjahan killed two brothers, two nephews and two cousins. One day, his four sons would battle in the same way and he would watch three of them die.

Books You Can Read

1. *Nurjahan* by Ellison Banks Findly; Oxford University Press
2. *The Great Mughals* by Bamber Gascoine; Dorset Press, New York
3. *The Great Mughals* by Abraham Eraly; Penguin